THIS BOOK BELONGS TO:

....

....

....

....

Once Upon a
UNICORN'S
HORN

BEATRICE BLUE

CLARION BOOKS | Houghton Mifflin Harcourt | Boston New York

ONCE upon a magic forest,
there was a little girl named June.

June knew the woods were
full of treasures waiting
to be discovered.

She loved to climb
the tallest trees
to find castles,

and peer through the bushes
to find magic wands.

Then, one day, June found the
greatest treasure of all . . .

. . . tiny magic horses learning to fly!
June couldn't believe it.

They shook their soft fur,

fluttered their sparkly tails,

and whizzed into the air.

But there was one little horse that wasn't flying.
He looked very sad.

"Are you okay, little horsie?"
June asked. "Can't you fly?"

He shook his head.

"I can help you," said June. "We just have to make your fur shake and your tail flutter."

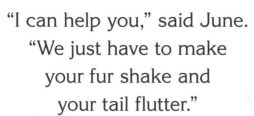

So they tried rolling,

and jumping,

and running really fast,

but nothing happened.

"I guess we'll have to use magic,"
said June.

She rummaged through her box of treasures
until she found her most powerful magic wand.

June swooshed a big swoosh
and wished a big wish . . .

. . . but it still didn't work.
The little horse was sadder than ever,

and so was June.

As soon as she got home, Mom and Dad
could tell something was wrong. Not even
her favorite dinner could make her smile.

June told them all about the tiny horse.

"I tried to help, but my magic wand didn't work,"
she said. "I think it's broken."

"Don't worry," Mom and Dad said.
"We can fix it together!"

"How?" asked June.

"Let's start by trying to cheer up your friend," said Mom.

"Tomorrow we'll think of all the things that a little horse might like," said Dad.

The next morning,
everyone thought hard.

"Something sweet?"
asked June.

"Something happy?"
asked Dad.

"What about something
to share?" asked Mom.

"I know," said June.
"Let's give him an
ice cream cone!"

Just before she left, Mom and Dad
whispered some magic words to make sure
the ice cream tasted super sweet.

June couldn't wait to
cheer up her friend.

She ran as fast as she could,

but it was a little too fast.

She tripped, then the ice cream
slipped out of her hand, and . . .

It was a disaster.

But then June saw that the little horse liked his new horn very much.

He smiled,
then he laughed,

then he shook his soft fur and fluttered
his sparkly tail . . .

. . . and it worked!

It was the happiest day ever.

And ever since, magic horses
have been called unicorns,

for they all wear horns to remember the day when a little girl was a good friend.

June often wears one too, and she never forgets the magic words.

MY MAGIC IS DEEP INSIDE.

I DON'T NEED A WAND TO FLY.

To Mum and Dad,
who showed me where to find magic.

Big thanks and love to Dani, Ali, Zoë, and Katie for
the huge help and encouragement.

CLARION BOOKS
3 Park Avenue
New York, New York 10016

Copyright © 2019 by Beatrice Blue

First published in the U.K. in 2019 by Frances Lincoln Children's Books,
an imprint of Quarto Publishing Place,
The Old Brewery, 6 Blundell Street, London N7 9BH

First published in the United States in 2020.

Clarion Books is an imprint of Houghton Mifflin Harcourt Publishing Company.

hmhbooks.com

The illustrations in this book were created digitally.
The text was set in ITC Korinna Std.

Library of Congress Cataloging-in-Publication Data
Names: Blue, Beatrice, 1991– author, illustrator.
Title: Once upon a unicorn's horn / Beatrice Blue.
Description: Boston ; New York : Clarion Books, Houghton Mifflin Harcourt,
[2020] | Summary: A little girl befriends a sad, tiny horse, and with a
little magic (and an ice cream cone), helps him fly.
Identifiers: LCCN 2019015728 | ISBN 9780358229261 (hardcover picture book)
Subjects: | CYAC: Unicorns—Fiction. | Friendship—Fiction. | Magic—Fiction.
Classification: LCC PZ7.1.B6435 On 2020 | DDC [E]—dc23
LC record available at https://lccn.loc.gov/2019015728

Manufactured in China
TOP 10 9 8 7 6 5 4 3 2 1
4500764931